Pete the Cat

Go, Pete, Go!

by
James Dean

HARPER FESTIVAL
An Imprint of HarperCollinsPublishers

Harperfestival is an imprint of HarperCollins Publishers.

Pete the Cat: Go, Pete, Go!

For information address HarperCollins Children's Books, a division of HarperCollins Publishers,
195 Broadway, New York, NY 10007.
www.harpercollinschildrens.com
ISBN 978-0-06-264102-1

The artist used pen and ink, with watercolor and acrylic paint,
on 300lb hot press paper to create the illustrations for this book.
18   19   20   21   LEO   10   9   8   7   6   5   4   3
❖
July 2018

It's a beautiful day, and Pete the Cat has decided to take his bike for a ride. Nothing makes Pete happier than feeling the sun on his fur and the breeze on his face.

Vroom! Vroom!

Turtle has a new race car. "Who wants to have a race?" he says.

"Not me," says Grumpy Toad.
"My motorcycle has a flat tire."

"Not me," says Emma.
"My car is too old and slow."

"Not me," says Callie.
"My bus is a work of art.
It's not meant for racing."

"I'll race you," says Pete, knowing how much Turtle likes to race.

"But your bike has no motor," says Turtle. "My race car is super quick. I'll win for sure."

"That's okay," says Pete. "I just want to try my best and have fun."

Everyone is excited for the big race.

"On your mark. Get set. Go!" Callie shouts.

Turtle steps on the gas pedal and—vroom!—zooms away.

Pete waves good-bye
and then pedals off.

Pete sees Turtle up ahead. Turtle slows down to let Pete catch up.

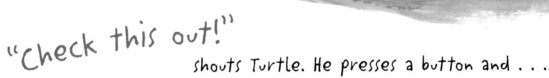

"Check this out!" shouts Turtle. He presses a button and . . .

... Fins appear!

Now Turtle's race car goes even faster.

Vrrroom! Vrrroom!

Pete's bike doesn't have fins, but he does have a basket.
He stops and takes out a tasty red apple.

Nothing is better than a tasty red apple on a beautiful day.

Turtle sees that Pete is WAY behind. He spies a diner up ahead. "Might as well grab a bite to eat," Turtle says as he pulls into a parking spot.

"Yum!" says Turtle, eating a grilled-cheese sandwich. He is in no rush. He is sure he will win the race.

"Dessert?" the waitress asks. "Don't mind if I do," Turtle says.

While Turtle finishes his lunch, Pete continues pedaling. The sun is high and the breeze is blowing. It's a beautiful day for a race.

Pete sees Turtle leaving the diner. Pete waves hello, but Turtle doesn't wave back. Turtle just jumps in his car and peels off.

"I guess he didn't see me." Pete shrugs.

But Turtle did see Pete. He knows that Pete isn't going to give up easily.

So Turtle presses a button and his tires inflate into mag wheels that let him swerve around the curves at top speed!

vrrr-vrrr-vrrrooooom!

Pete passes a rosebush as he goes around a curve. Pete knows he should keep racing, but he can't resist.

The roses are just so beautiful. . . . He has to stop to smell them.

Turtle sees that he has a HUGE lead.
He knows he's going to win.

LEMONADE

He stops for a nice,
cold glass of lemonade, and that's when
he sees the hammock hanging between
two trees. He's exhausted from racing so fast.
He figures a quick nap will help him in the home stretch.

Pete pedals past and sees Turtle sleeping. That's cool, Pete thinks as he rides by as quietly as he can. "Turtle must really be tired. I'm glad he's getting some rest."

Grumpy Toad finds Turtle fast asleep!

"Wake up, Turtle," says Grumpy Toad. "If you don't get back in the race, Pete is going to win."

"That's impossible," says Turtle,
thinking it must be a joke.
But it's no joke!

Turtle presses a button and rocket boosters appear, making him go super-duper fast.

Vrrrrrrooooooooooooom!

But by the time Turtle nears the finish line . . .

... Pete has already won the race!

"How did you do it?" Turtle asks.
"Slow and steady," says Pete. "Maybe next time instead of racing, we can ride together."
"Great idea," says Turtle.